Me Too!

I Like to Read® books, created by award-winning picture book artists as well as talented newcomers, instill confidence and the joy of reading in new readers.

We want to hear every new reader say, "I like to read!"

———————————————————————

Visit our website for flash cards, activities, and more about the series:
www.holidayhouse.com/ILiketoRead
#ILTR

This book has been tested by an educational expert and determined to be a guided reading level C.

Me Too!

Valeri Gorbachev

I Like to Read®

HOLIDAY HOUSE • NEW YORK

"I love snow!" said Bear.
"Me too!" said Chipmunk.

"I will dig," said Bear.
"Me too!" said Chipmunk.

"I will make a snowman,"
said Bear.
"Me too!" said Chipmunk.

"I like our snowman," said Bear.
"Me too!" said Chipmunk.

"I want to skate," said Bear.
"Me too!" said Chipmunk.

"I fell!" said Bear.
"Me too!" said Chipmunk.

"I love to ski!" said Bear.
"Me too!" said Chipmunk.

"The snow is deep," said Bear.
"It is up to my knees."
"Mine too!" said Chipmunk.

"Let's go home," said Bear.
"I am cold."
"Me too!" said Chipmunk.

"I had fun in the snow," said Bear.

"Me too!" said Chipmunk.

"Sweet dreams," said Bear.

"You too!" said Chipmunk.

Copyright © 2013 by Valeri Gorbachev
All Rights Reserved
HOLIDAY HOUSE is registered in the U.S. Patent and Trademark Office.
Printed and Bound in November 2018 at Tien Wah Press, Johor Bahru, Johor, Malaysia.
The artwork was created with watercolor and ink.
www.holidayhouse.com
5 7 9 10 8 6

Library of Congress Cataloging-in-Publication Data
Gorbachev, Valeri.
Me too! / by Valeri Gorbachev. — 1st ed.
p. cm. — (I like to read)
Summary: "Chipmunk and Bear spend a snowy day together and
discover that they like to do all of the same things."
— Provided by publisher.
ISBN 978-0-8234-2744-4 (hardcover)
[1. Snow—Fiction. 2. Chipmunks—Fiction. 3. Bears—Fiction.] I. Title.
PZ7.G6475Me 2013
[E]—dc23
2012039294

ISBN 978-0-8234-3179-3 (paperback)

I Like to Read® Books
You will like all of them!

Boy, Bird, and Dog by David McPhail

Car Goes Far by Michael Garland

Come Back, Ben by John Hassett and Ann Hassett

Dinosaurs Don't, Dinosaurs Do by Steve Björkman

Fireman Fred by Lynn Rowe Reed

Fish Had a Wish by Michael Garland

The Fly Flew In by David Catrow

Happy Cat by Steve Henry

I Have a Garden by Bob Barner

I Will Try by Marilyn Janovitz

Late Nate in a Race by Emily Arnold McCully

The Lion and the Mice
by Rebecca Emberley and Ed Emberley

Look! by Ted Lewin

Me Too! by Valeri Gorbachev

Mice on Ice
by Rebecca Emberley and Ed Emberley

Pete Won't Eat by Emily Arnold McCully

Pig Has a Plan by Ethan Long

Sam and the Big Kids by Emily Arnold McCully

See Me Dig by Paul Meisel

See Me Run by Paul Meisel
A THEODOR SEUSS GEISEL AWARD HONOR BOOK

Sick Day by David McPhail

What Am I? Where Am I? by Ted Lewin

You Can Do It! by Betsy Lewin

Visit holidayhouse.com to read more
about I Like to Read® Books.

I Like to Read® Books in Paperback
You will like all of them!

Boy, Bird, and Dog by David McPhail

Car Goes Far by Michael Garland

Come Back, Ben by Ann Hassett and John Hassett

Dinosaurs Don't, Dinosaurs Do by Steve Björkman

Fireman Fred by Lynn Rowe Reed

Fish Had a Wish by Michael Garland

The Fly Flew In by David Catrow

Happy Cat by Steve Henry

I Have a Garden by Bob Barner

I Will Try by Marilyn Janovitz

Late Nate in a Race by Emily Arnold McCully

The Lion and the Mice by Rebecca Emberley and Ed Emberley

Look! by Ted Lewin

Me Too! by Valeri Gorbachev

Mice on Ice by Rebecca Emberley and Ed Emberley

Pete Won't Eat by Emily Arnold McCully

Pig Has a Plan by Ethan Long

Sam and the Big Kids by Emily Arnold McCully

See Me Dig by Paul Meisel

See Me Run by Paul Meisel
A THEODOR SEUSS GEISEL AWARD HONOR BOOK

Sick Day by David McPhail

What Am I? Where Am I? by Ted Lewin

You Can Do It! by Betsy Lewin

Visit http://www.holidayhouse.com/I-Like-to-Read/ for more
about I Like to Read® books, including flash cards,
reproducibles, and the complete list of titles.